P9-AGH-109

MAN GAVE NAMES TO ALL THE ANIMALS

by Bob Dylan

ILLUSTRATED BY JIM ARNOSKY

STERLING CHILDREN'S BOOKS
New York

"And God formed out of the earth all the wild beasts and all the birds of the sky, and brought them to the man to see what he would call them; and whatever the man called each living creature, that would be its name. And the man gave names to all the cattle and to the birds of the sky and to all the wild beasts . . ."

Genesis 2: 19–20

Man gave names to all the animals

In the beginning, in the beginning.

Man gave names to all the animals

In the beginning, long time ago.

He saw an animal that liked to growl,

Big furry paws and he liked to howl,

Great big furry back and furry hair.

Man gave names to all the animals

In the beginning, in the beginning.

Man gave names to all the animals

In the beginning, long time ago.

He saw an animal up on a hill

Chewing up so much grass until she was filled.

He saw milk comin' out but he didn't know how.

"Ah, think I'll call it a COW."

Man gave names to all the animals

In the beginning, in the beginning.

Man gave names to all the animals

In the beginning, long time ago.

He saw an animal that liked to snort,
Horns on his head and they weren't too short.

It looked like there wasn't
nothin' that he couldn't pull.

"Ah, think I'll call it a *bull*."

Man gave names to all the animals

In the beginning, in the beginning.

Man gave names to all the animals

In the beginning, long time ago.

He saw an animal leavin' a muddy trail,

Real dirty face and a curly tail.

He wasn't too small and he wasn't too big.

"Ah, think I'll call it a *Pig*."

Man gave names to all the animals

In the beginning, in the beginning.

Man gave names to all the animals

In the beginning, long time ago.

Next animal that he did meet

Had wool on his back and hooves on his feet,

Eating grass on a mountainside so steep.

"Ah, think I'll call it a SHEEP."

Man gave names to all the animals

In the beginning, in the beginning.

Man gave names to all the animals

In the beginning, long time ago.

He saw an animal as smooth as glass

Slithering his way through the grass.

Saw him disappear by a tree near a lake . . .

Can you find all of these creatures within the pages of this book?
Some appear more than once. All together,
there are more than 170 animals to find!

baby crane	green parrot	plover
baby swan	hornbill	pronghorn
bald eagle	horse	purple gallinule
bat	howler monkey	red macaw
bird of paradise	ibex	red-tailed hawk
black bear	ibis	rhinoceros
black-necked stilt	iguana	ring-necked pheasant
blue macaw	jack	rooster
brown pelican	jaguar	ruby-throated hummingbird
buffalo	java monkey	sailfish
bull	kangaroo	salmon
bumblebee	kestrel	sandhill crane
burro	kudu	scissortail
calf	lemur	snake
camel	leopard	snow goose
caribou	lion	sparrow
carp	little blue heron	spider
catfish	long nose gar	squirrel monkey
cheetah	macaque monkey	sunfish
chimpanzee	mandrill	swallow
cockatoo	marsh hawk	swallowtail butterfly
cow	monarch butterfly	swan
crocodile	mountain sheep	tiger
dolphin	mourning dove	tiger shark
dragonfly	mullet	toucan
elephant	night heron	turkey vulture
fiddler crab	orangutan	vermillion snapper
finch	orca	walrus
flamingo	oryx	white-tailed deer
gibbon	ostrich	whooping crane
giraffe	owl	wild pig
gorilla	peacock bass	wood duck
great blue heron	penguin	woodpecker
green heron	pintail duck	zebra

If you need clues, visit www.jimarnosky.com.

To Colleen and Chris.
—J. A.

STERLING CHILDREN'S BOOKS
New York

An Imprint of Sterling Publishing Co., Inc.
1166 Avenue of the Americas
New York, NY 10036

STERLING CHILDREN'S BOOKS and the distinctive Sterling Children's Books logo
are trademarks of Sterling Publishing Co., Inc.

Text/lyrics © 1979 Special Rider Music
Illustrations and introduction © 2010 Jim Arnosky

All rights reserved. No part of this publication may be reproduced, stored in a retrieval system,
or transmitted in any form or by any means (including electronic, mechanical, photocopying,
recording, or otherwise) without prior written permission from the publisher.

ISBN 978-1-4549-3788-3

Library of Congress Cataloging-in-Publication Data

Dylan, Bob.
Man gave names to all the animals / by Bob Dylan ;
illustrated by Jim Arnosky.
p. cm.
Summary: Based on a song by Bob Dylan, tells the story of how man
named the animals of the world.
1. Children's songs--United States--Texts. [1. Songs. 2.
Animals--Songs and music.] I. Arnosky, Jim, ill. II. Title.
PZ8.3.D985Man 2010
782.42--dc22
[E]
2009030717

For information about custom editions, special sales, and premium and corporate purchases, please contact
Sterling Special Sales at 800-805-5489 or specialsales@sterlingpublishing.com.

Manufactured in China

Lot #:
2 4 6 8 10 9 7 5 3 1
06/19

sterlingpublishing.com

Design by Kate Moll
Calligraphy by Georgia Deaver
The artwork for this book was prepared using pencil and acrylic paints.

101927.4K1/B1453/A3